minedition

North American edition published 2020 by minedition, New York

Text Copyright © 2020 Thodoris Papaioannou
Illustrationen Copyright © 2020 Petros Bouloubasis
Coproduction with Michael Neugebauer Publishing Ltd., Hong Kong.
Rights arranged with "minedition ag", Zurich, Switzerland. All rights reserved.
This book, or parts thereof, may not be reproduced in any form without permission
in writing from the publisher.
The scanning, uploading and distribution of this book via the Internet or via any other
means without the permission of the publisher is illegal and punishable by law.
Please purchase only authorized electronic editions, and do not participate in or encourage
electronic piracy of copyrighted materials. Your support of the author's rights is appreciated.
Michael Neugebauer Publishing Ltd.,
19 West 21st Street, #1201, New York, NY 10010
e-mail: info@minedition.com
This book was printed in May 2020 at Hong Kong Discovery Printing Company Limited.
3/F., Blue Box Factory Building, 25 Hing Wo Street, Tin Wan, Aberdeen, Hong Kong, China
Typesetting in Papyrus
Library of Congress Cataloging-in-Publication Data available upon request.

ISBN 978-1-6626-5005-5
10 9 8 7 6 5 4 3 2 1
First Impression

For more information please visit our website: www.minedition.com

Thodoris Papaioannou **While You're Away**

Petros Bouloubasis

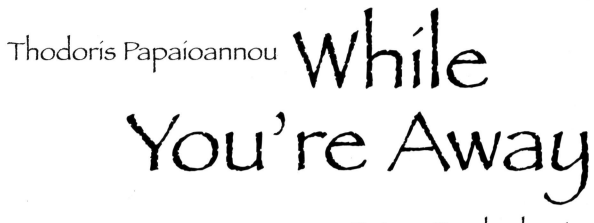

minedition

While you're away from the forest a mother doe might be searching for tasty blueberries to feed her fawn for breakfast.

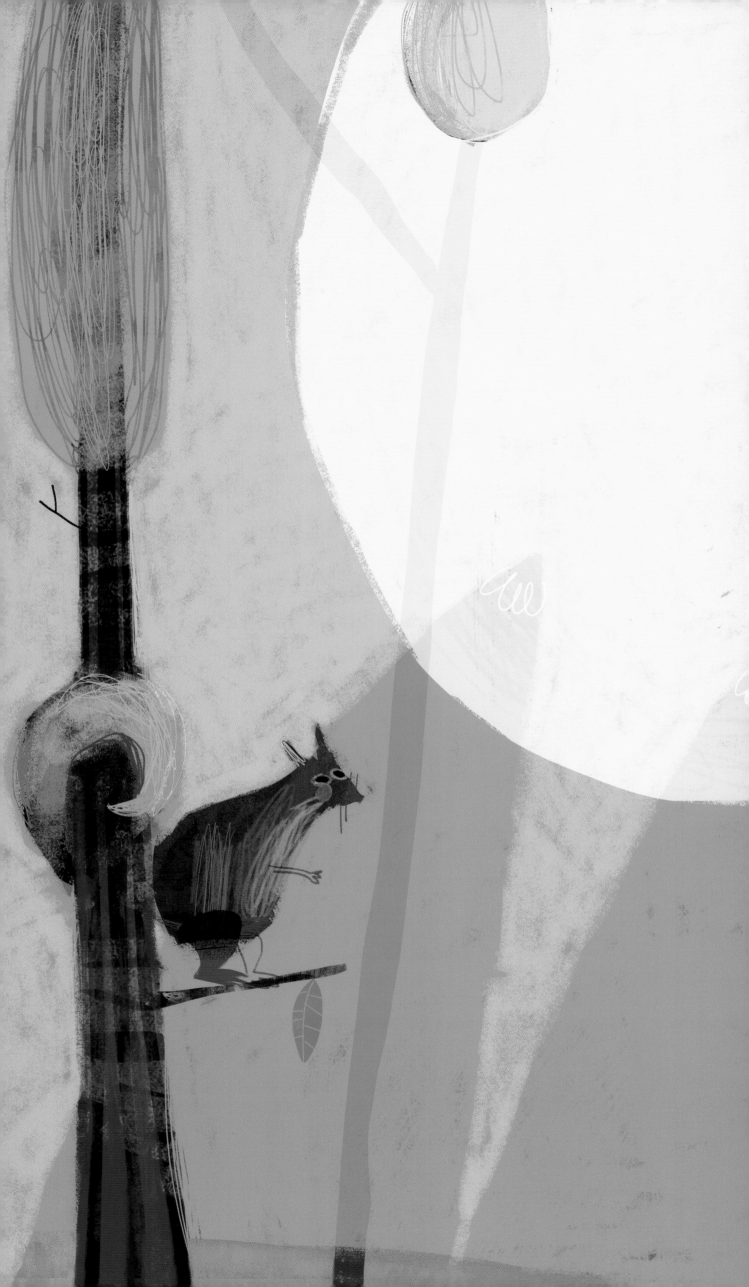

A squirrel might be getting ready
for the leap of its life to a tree
where its sweetheart waits.

A lazy lizard might be lying among wild strawberries, enjoying the sun's warm rays.

A fox, tired after an all-night hunt,
might be fast asleep,
cuddled up with her babies.

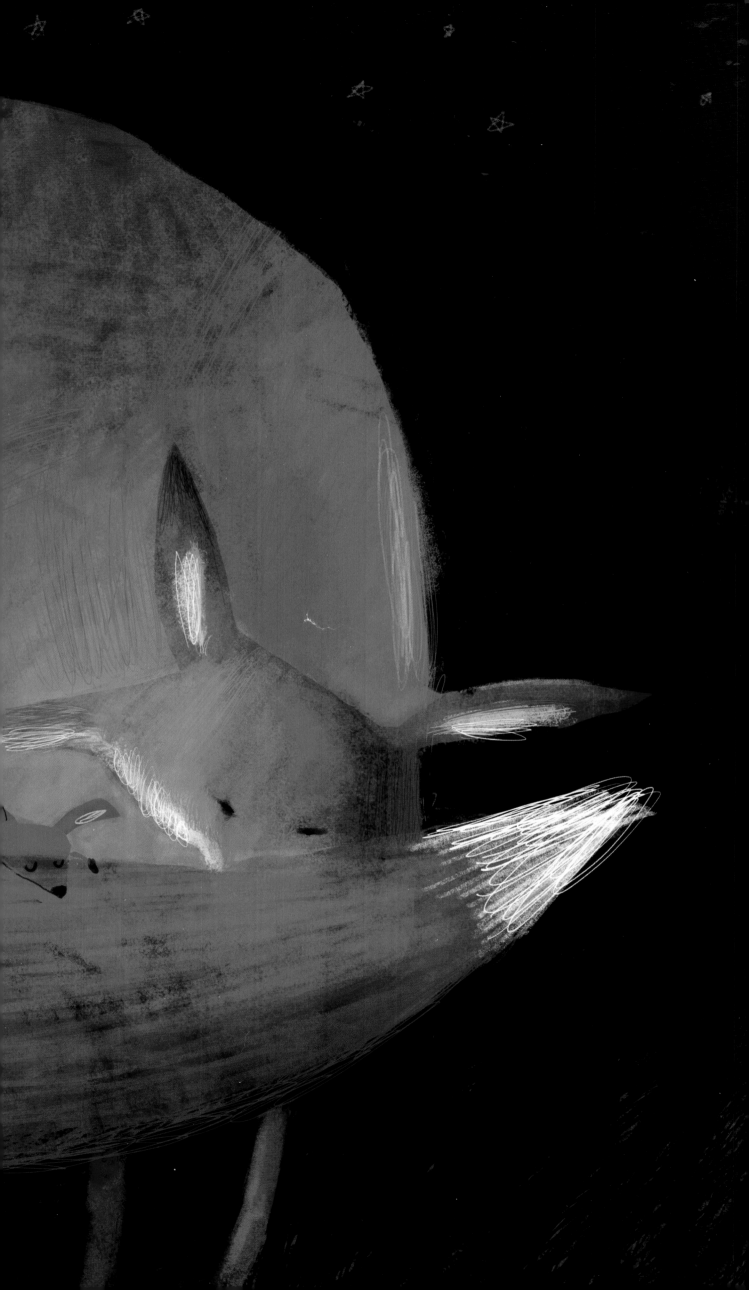

While you're away from the river
two bears might be quenching their
thirst after eating too much honey.

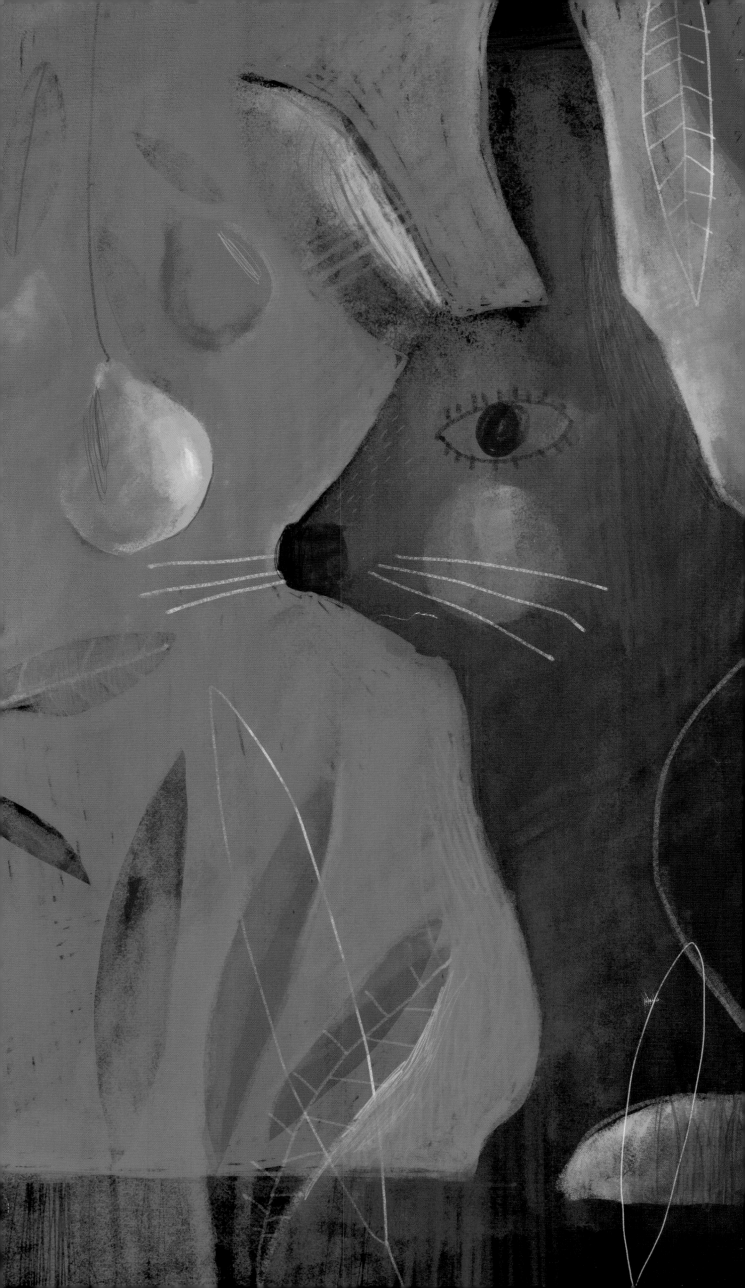

A rabbit might be nibbling on wild pears.

A tree snake might be shedding
its skin, somewhere behind the rocks.

A hedgehog might be scampering through the fallen
leaves, carrying wild berries on its prickly spines.

While you're away from
the lake a dragonfly might be taking
a midday bath near the waterfall.

A hoopoe might be joyfully singing, for it has just finished building its nest.

An owl might be standing still in the
dense green foliage, unseen for hours.

The morning sun might be waking up
the first wildflowers of spring.

Though you might not be there to
witness them, these small miracles
happen every day.

But if you ever happen
    to be there and paying attention...
    Shh! Just keep still and quiet!

You might be lucky enough to see
life's everyday wonders,
whenever you're not away.